Scary Fairy
in Wicked Wood

Kind World Publishing, PO Box 22356, Eagan, MN 55122
www.kindworldpublishing.com
© 2022 by Kind World Publishing
All Rights Reserved

First published in North America in 2022 by Kind World Publishing.

Originally published in Slovenia by KUD Sodobnost International,
(www.sodobnost.com, sodobnost@guest.arnes.si), Ljubljana
Original Title: Groznovilca v Hudi hosti.

Text © Jana Bauer, 2011
Illustrations © Caroline Thaw, 2011
Translated by David Limon

The book is published with the financial support of the Slovenian Book Agency.

ISBN:978-1-63894-004-3 (hardcover)
ISBN: 978-1-63894-010-4 (ebook)

Library of Congress Cataloging-in-Publication Data is available on the
Library of Congress website.
Library of Congress Control Number: 2021924217

Printed in the United States of America.

Jana Bauer

Scary Fairy
in Wicked Wood

Illustrated by **Caroline Thaw**
Translated by **David Limon**

PUBLISHING

Eagan, Minnesota

Scary Fairy Comes to Wicked Wood

One cloudy Saturday something strange was seen flying towards Wicked Wood. Something really strange.

"An asteroid!" gasped Squirrel as she looked at the sky. "And it's heading straight for us!" She ran directly to Owl's place. "Asteroid!" she kept shouting.

"Really?" asked Bear, who happened to be sipping tea with Owl.

"Asteroid!" Squirrel frantically waved her little paw towards the sky.

Owl looked up, alarmed. "What could it be?"

"Certainly not a bird," muttered Bear, staring at the funny object in the sky. "Nor a frog nor a mouse. Nor a mole for that matter."

"Strange," Owl agreed.

"I'm telling you—it's an asteroid!" shrieked Squirrel.

"And asteroids have stupid habits. They smash you to s-m-i-t-h-e-r-e-e-n-s!"

Terrified out of her wits, Squirrel ran off.

"It looks like a pear," volunteered Bear. "A pear carrying a hedgehog."

"But," Owl objected, "are pears really so colorful, and hedgehogs so much . . . ?"

"Like teapots?" Bear helped out.

As the object came nearer, they both agreed it was a balloon, a small, patched-up balloon with a teapot instead of a basket.

The balloon began to descend. As the teapot touched the ground, the South Wind dragged it across the roots sticking out of the soil. It sounded like this: BOOOMF. BOOOMF. BAAAMF! Inside the teapot someone started to curse: "Ouch, that hurts! Stop that, South Wind! HRRRAAAAGH. You're wicked!" And then: SQUEEAAL. PLINK PLONK. The balloon soon got tangled in a bramble and the teapot finally came to rest. The lid opened with a clatter and out climbed a little creature. Frowning. Quite mad. In a summer dress and with a little cap from which grew forklike horns.

"I'll remember that." The little creature shook her fist at the wind, which was making the treetops seesaw this way and that. "You're lucky it was me in the teapot and not my grandmother. I bet you wouldn't dare toss her about like that. She'd grab you by the tail and untie all your knots!"

The little one straightened her dress, checked her antlers, and thought of her grandmother with her china cups.

"That's exactly what she did to the North Wind, if you want to know. And only because it blew a little bit of tobacco from her pipe. Did you hear that? Just a little bit of tobacco!"

"It's one of those scary fairies," Owl said to Bear under the pine tree. "I don't remember why exactly, but they seem to be at odds with the winds."

The little creature pulled a bundle of colorful things from the teapot and rummaged among them until she found a gold coin. Then she looked for the nearest fern and began to dig a hole beneath it.

"What's she doing?" asked Bear.

"Burying a gold coin," explained Owl. "Scary fairies keep moving their gold coins around the wood."

"Shall we go and say hello?" Bear suggested.

"She won't stay," Owl screeched and flew into the sky. "They can't bear to be without their aunts, cousins, sisters and grandmas for very long."

Bear shrugged and trundled off.

Scary Fairy continued to shout and threaten and spit on the ground. Then she noticed a hole midway up the trunk of a beech tree.

"That'll be my home," she said, delighted. With the heavy bundle on her back she climbed the trunk. Then she hung the bundle on the nearest branch and clambered in the hole.

"Not enough room," she informed the hazelnuts as she chucked them out one by one. Satisfied, she reached for her bundle. Just then the South Wind blew from behind the tree and threw her things to the ground. The bundle burst open and her possessions were strewn all over the place. Her lucky blue button landed under an oak tree and her little mirrors came to rest under a pine tree.

"Wiiiiiiind!" shrieked Scary Fairy. She was hopping mad. She cracked her knuckles and gritted her teeth, howling and screaming the whole time.

Hedgehog came shuffling along. "Who's making that dreadful racket?" he muttered in annoyance.

"Hey!" he shouted as he spotted the teapot. "Anyone in there?"

Scary Fairy scampered up to Hedgehog the moment she saw him.

"I haven't combed my hair yet today," she said. She grabbed Hedgehog and prickled her hair with him.

Hedgehog was silent at first, but then he got mad.

"Some manners would do you no harm, girl!" he shouted at her. "I'm a hedgehog, not a brush for your matted hair."

Scary Fairy did not reply. She collected her little mirrors and admired her new prickly hairdo.

"Neither would please and thank you," Hedgehog ranted on, "but I suppose your mom never taught you that."

"My grandmother," said the little one, "has seventeen hedgehogs in her drawer for combing her hair. One for each day of the month. They're all terribly impolite. Probably because she feeds them prunes. Which are known to cause impoliteness."

Hedgehog tried to figure out if each month really did have seventeen days.

"Luckily, I don't like prunes at all," continued the little creature. "I'd like to comb my hair with you every evening, so come to my tree hole when it gets dark. And please don't be late!"

Hedgehog was speechless. To treat a grown-up hedgehog like that! He couldn't decide whether to prick the little one or report her behavior to Owl. Furious, he stormed off.

Scary Fairy tramped off deeper into the wood, leaving her possessions lying around on the ground. Serves them right, she thought. The wood was silent and beautiful. She came across some excellent puddles. She decided she would come back and check them out in the moonlight.

Happy that the teapot had landed in such an unusual forest, she returned to the beech tree. She collected some twigs and made them into a flight of stairs leading up to her hole. She planted some pumpkins and decorative toadstools. She hung a swing in front of the hole. Out of the teapot she dragged an armchair, which she had managed to steal from her grandmother. Exhausted, she sank into it. She reached for a pencil, intending to write in her diary, "Dear diary, I've found a new home. Here they have disagreeable hedgehogs and first-rate puddles."

But the diary wasn't there! She searched inside and outside the hole. Nothing. Once again she started to shriek, howl, crack her knuckles and grind her teeth.

Owl came flying through the treetops.

"Why is there so much noise?" she asked.

"Someone stole my diary," yelled Scary Fairy.

"Not in a thousand years," said Salamander, who was hiding under a leaf.

"Completely impossible," added Earthworm, who happened to be crawling past.

"There are no thieves in Wicked Wood," explained Bear, who came sauntering from behind the pine tree.

"It's been stolen," insisted Scary Fairy. "I've searched every square inch of the ground. Nothing! I've looked under every pine cone. Nothing! So?"

Owl thought a while.

"A little earlier, Hedgehog came to report you," she said. "He claimed that you have no manners."

"Hedgehogs are soooo stupid," replied Scary Fairy. "All I did was comb my hair with him, and he kicked up such a fuss."

"Did you ask his permission?" Owl inquired.

"Did I what?" shouted Scary Fairy.

Owl sighed. There will be trouble with this one, she thought.

Bear suggested they knock on Hedgehog's door, and they all agreed.

"What is it?" yelled Hedgehog angrily, as he opened his door.

"Have you seen Scary Fairy's diary?" Owl asked.

"Seen it, taken it, read it," snapped Hedgehog.

"What?!" Scary Fairy exploded, jumping up and down.

"You've read my diary? Without my permission?"

"And I had to beg you to comb your hair with me, I suppose!" Hedgehog snapped.

Owl suggested that he return the diary.

"All my secrets are in there," said Scary Fairy, outraged.

"I understand why you're upset," Bear tried to console her.

Scary Fairy stormed off. Hedgehog whispered to Dormouse: "I had to read it to see if she was dangerous."

"And?" Dormouse was all ears.

"You wouldn't believe it," Hedgehog replied, "but her grandmother can knock a pear off a tree just by spitting at it."

Scary Fairy and the Magic Sand

On that cloudy Saturday night all the animals were
sleeping soundly in their holes and dens. Only Salamander
was feeling unhappy, because he and Snail had quarreled.
Then the clouds were blown away by a sudden wind and
moonlight shone into the wood among the giant oak trees.
Scary Fairy woke up, climbed out of bed, put on a pair of
neat little boots and went off to jump in puddles.

She stumbled across a particularly good puddle. "Wow!"
she said to herself. She jumped in, splashed about and
continued her muddy dance until early morning. Only at
dawn, when the first light colored the Sunday sky, did she set

off back to her tree hole. Next to a deep pool halfway home she noticed a sign:

MAGIC SAND! KEEP AWAY!!

Scary Fairy immediately climbed into the pool. The sand was black and wet and it smelled of Colorado beetles. Scary Fairy stuffed a fistful of it into her purse. Then she went home.

Hedgehog, Dormouse and Squirrel had been waiting for her in front of her tree hole since early morning. Hedgehog had not forgotten the insult of being mistaken for a common hairbrush. He had dragged Dormouse with him in the hope that together they could persuade Scary Fairy to apologize. Squirrel was there for a different reason: the hole in which Scary Fairy had set up home was in fact hers. It's true that she didn't actually live there, but so what?

"You can't just take somewhere over like that," Squirrel kept muttering, ready for a fight if necessary. "You can't move into someone's property without paying rent."

"That's right," said Hedgehog. Dormouse merely yawned.

"Fine," agreed Scary Fairy. She opened her purse and sprinkled a pinch of black sand into Squirrel's paw.

"Toss this over your hazelnuts and they will multiply."

Squirrel, satisfied, clenched her fist and hopped off home.

"And what about me?" Hedgehog stretched out his paw, thinking she might offer him something to magically multiply his pear. "There is no such thing as free hairdressing, you know."

Scary Fairy gave some black sand to him as well. Without checking or even smelling it, Hedgehog darted home.

"Me too," begged Dormouse. He was thinking of rubbing the magic dust into his fur so that it would grow thicker.

19

"You?" said Scary Fairy. "I don't owe you anything."

"Yes you do," insisted Dormouse. "Just imagine how early I had to get up. And while we waited for you I had to put up with Hedgehog, who wouldn't stop farting because pears give him wind!"

"Alright," agreed Scary Fairy. She gave him some sand and shut herself up in her hole.

The
following
morning Bear,
quite out of breath,
knocked on Owl's door. "Auntie,
help, Dormouse has gone mad!"
Dormouse at that moment came
rushing out from behind a tree. He
was waving a dry twig as if it was a
gun. He was digging holes in the
ground and setting traps in the belief that he was a hunter.

"Completely nuts," Owl agreed with Bear as they watched Dormouse attack a fox.

The fox escaped unhurt but only because Bear intervened.

"We'll have to put him away," Owl said.

But no sooner had they stuffed Dormouse into a disused hole in the ground than a new racket began in Wicked Wood.

"Squirrel!" Bear pointed out.

"Oh my, oh my!" Squirrel yelled. "The end is nigh! My hazelnuts have gone mad. They want to swallow me up!"

She was right. An army of hopping hazelnuts was chasing
Squirrel. Owl, like Bear, had no idea what was happening.
But clearly Squirrel had to be helped.

"The traps!" remembered Owl.

And so Squirrel was saved from her own hazelnuts by
the traps set earlier by Dormouse. Every single one of them
was soon caught. Squirrel, clearly shaken, couldn't stop
whimpering.

No sooner had Owl and Bear calmed her down than the
racket resumed. This time it was Hedgehog. He was wailing
in his hole and refused to come out.

"Don't be a wimp," Bear coaxed him. "Come on out."

But Hedgehog refused. Finally he relented a little and
opened the window. Bear and Owl recoiled in shock. All
Hedgehog's needles had turned into daisies.

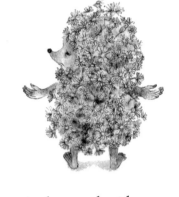

"Never again," he lamented, "will I
be able to bring home a pear. I'll die of
hunger if I don't die of shame first."

How queer, Owl thought as
Hedgehog continued:

"It's Scary Fairy's fault. She gave me magic dust and said
that my pear would multiply if I sprinkled some over it. And
that's what I did. Then I stuck the pear on my needles and
rushed home. And now this!"

"Magic dust?" it suddenly dawned on Owl. "Was it
black?"

"It was," Hedgehog nodded.

"Did it stink? Was it wet?"

"Both," Hedgehog confirmed.

"Did Dormouse and Squirrel get some too?"

Hedgehog nodded.

"Magic sand," Owl and Bear said together. "Hedgehog,
come along," Owl beckoned.

"In this state?" objected Hedgehog. "Never!"

"But why," Owl asked angrily, "did you even want more pears? Are you not happy with one?"

Hedgehog fell silent and followed them.

Owl knocked on Scary Fairy's window. She had to knock twice before the little creature sleepily opened the door.

"Listen," Owl began. "What you did to Dormouse, Squirrel and Hedgehog is simply unacceptable. You'll have to acquire some manners."

"No, thank you," Scary Fairy yawned. "I much prefer mulberry jelly."

"In our forest we help each other," Bear explained.

"That's your business," said Scary Fairy. "If you don't have any mulberry jelly for me I'll just go back to bed." She closed the window and locked the door.

"Well, what did I say?" muttered Hedgehog. "No manners to speak of."

"Wait for me here," said Owl, as she noticed Scary Fairy's little boots hanging on the nearest branch, and flew off.

It wasn't long before she was back. In her beak she carried some wet black sand. She dropped some into each of the boots.

Bear sighed. "I'm not sure this is the right way, Auntie."

"I'm sick and tired of having to ask and beg all the time," replied Owl.

Later that evening, as the moonlight broke through the tops of the old oak trees, a horrible yelling could be heard in Wicked Wood.

It was Scary Fairy. She wanted to jump barefoot in the moonlit puddles but couldn't take off her boots. No matter what she did, they just wouldn't come off. From behind a thick oak tree Bear appeared. He was followed by Owl, Hedgehog, Squirrel and others.

"Help me," begged Scary Fairy.

Bear shrugged. "But you wanted to be left alone."

"True, but you said that in your wood you help each other," replied Scary Fairy.

Owl and Bear looked at each other. Dormouse, glad to be a dormouse again, nodded. Squirrel, who didn't want

anyone to go through the ordeal she had gone through, did likewise. Only Hedgehog, half covered in needles and half still in daisies, kept staring at the ground.

"It's only magic sand," explained Owl. "The spell will break in a few hours."

"I know it's annoying," added Bear, "but until then your boots won't come off."

Scary Fairy looked unhappily at the beautiful muddy puddle and slowly tramped back to her tree hole.

Bear sighed.

Hedgehog leaned towards Dormouse and whispered: "You know, in that diary of hers I read that she's here because she was banished by her grandmother."

"That's not very nice!" Dormouse yawned.

Hedgehog looked at him sharply. "Dear Dormouse, perhaps you should ask yourself why her grandmother banished her. And how we're going to get rid of her!"

With an offended expression on his snout he pitter-pattered home.

Edgy Edgehog

On Wednesday at three in the afternoon Hedgehog knocked on Owl's door. "Just dropped in for tea," he said.

"Is that right?" Owl nodded and went to put the kettle on.

"Listen, Owl," Hedgehog began. "Have you noticed how things are not the same in Wicked Wood anymore?"

"Really?" Owl asked, looking perplexed.

"How things are more and more like they never were? And less and less like they used to be?" Hedgehog blabbered on. "And mark my words, things will never ever be the same again."

"Why don't you just say what you mean?" Owl lost her patience.

"Scary Fairy," Hedgehog muttered. "She must be sent away."

"Why?" Owl sighed.

"She romps about, disturbs the peace, corrupts the young and swears," Hedgehog recited his list of complaints.

"My dear Hedgehog," Owl said kindly. "Scary Fairy is a young, boisterous, frightened little thing. Where can we send her? Home? You should hear how terribly her grandmother swears! No, Hedgehog, Scary Fairy will stay

with us. We will try to show her that we like her. A few kind words and a warm paw here and there wouldn't do any harm."

"But—"

"May I count on you?"

"I can't just—"

"Hedgehog?"

"Umfff," mumbled Hedgehog, then he drank his chamomile tea and left.

Filled with dark thoughts, he arrived at Dormouse's place and banged on the door. Strangely enough, Dormouse wasn't asleep. He was in fact on his way out.

"Dormouse," Hedgehog whispered, "we must get rid of Scary Fairy. But not a word to anyone. We'll do it alone."

"Don't be silly," Dormouse said. "Whatever for?"

"Because she is potty," Hedgehog lost his cool. "Potty! Black sand and all that. And all those hedgehogs at her grandmother's! Don't tell me that isn't potty."

"She can be quite naughty," Dormouse conceded.

"Naughty? She corrupts the young," Hedgehog carried on. "As I was passing the pond the other day I heard the tadpoles swearing horribly. What next?"

"Old Frog swears horribly too. And you're lucky not to have heard Mother Frog! And you know what? They were swearing like that last month, when no one had even heard of Scary Fairy."

Hedgehog got so angry that he began to hiccup.

"You'll be, *hic*, terribly, *hic*, sorry, *hic*!" he blurted out and scurried home.

In front of his door he met Squirrel, who was heading somewhere.

"Listen, Squirrel, *hic*," Hedgehog began deviously, "do you know, *hic*, that Scary Fairy threw all your hazelnuts out of the tree hole? *Hic, hic.* Weren't you storing them for winter?"

"Now you tell me!" Squirrel squealed. "I completely forgot about them. How many? Twenty? Twenty-three? How many were there, Hedgehog? Tell me! If there were many, then poor Squirrel will starve this winter!"

"That's why something has to be done."

"You're right, Hedgehog," Squirrel nodded, "it has to be, but right now I have no time, as Squirrel and Dormouse have been invited to Scary Fairy's for tea."

And off she went.

Hedgehog was so struck by the news that his hiccups suddenly stopped. He slammed the door behind him and burrowed deep into the leaves of his rickety bed. There he huffed and puffed and plotted all night long.

Just before dawn an idea came to him. "I'll get rid of her!" he promised himself. "And I know how." He got out of bed and started to ransack his closet. "But what if it doesn't work." He paused for a brief moment. "No, it must work," he persuaded himself. He pulled an old woolen sock from the closet. He had inherited it from his maternal grandfather and was very fond of it. Even so, he made two holes in it for his eyes and pulled it over his head. "What else, what else?" he kept asking himself as he rummaged

inside the closet. He found a blue robe and two old pots. He put on the robe and shoved his paws inside the pots.

"I'm the terrible Edgy Edgehog!" he kept repeating to himself in a deep voice as he made his way through the brambles towards Scary Fairy's tree hole. He decided to add the word "Edgy" to make his character even more frightening. With all the gear on him and the two pots on his paws he barely managed to get as far as the beech tree. When he got there he banged the pots together until Scary Fairy opened her door.

"Who is making that racket?"

"Me!" Hedgehog roared. "I'm the terrible Edgy Edgehog and I've come to edgily eat you!"

"Oh terrible Edgehog, please don't," Scary Fairy squealed. "At least allow me to say goodbye to my friends."

Hedgehog said: "No goodbyes! But because I am good-hearted Edgy Edgehog I will edgily allow you to leave Wicked Wood now!"

"Good-hearted but terrifying Edgy Edgehog," said Scary Fairy, "let me just take my bundle and I'll be off. And thank you."

She darted inside. Hedgehog was almost sure that she had been quaking with fear. He returned home and for the first time in many days felt happy. "What a wonderful day!" he said.

33

He retired to his bed, exhausted but happy. He was about to close his eyes when he was overcome by a strange feeling that he wasn't alone. He looked towards the hearth. He was right. Someone was there, standing watching him.

"Dormouse, is that you?" Hedgehog asked nervously.

"No, it is me, the Terrible Horribilia," replied a bone-chilling voice.

"Are you going to eat me?" Hedgehog's voice trembled.

"I don't know if you're terribly tasty," replied Horribilia.

"F-for s-sure, of-f c-course I'm not," Hedgehog stuttered. "I-I have nee-needles and c-can get ho-horribly stick-stuck in y-your throat."

"I love needles," said the apparition. "But tell me before I eat you: am I terribly more horrible than Edgy Edgehog?"

"A thousand times," admitted Hedgehog.

"Yoo-hoo!" the creature squealed as the Terrible Horribilia changed into little Scary Fairy, letting the blanket in which she had been wrapped fall to the floor.

"I win, I win!" She danced around Hedgehog's bed. "You were so frightened! You were trembling like a leaf!"

"No I wasn't," Hedgehog refused to admit the obvious.

"Dear Hedgehog," Scary Fairy continued to dance around him, "you were so frightened you nearly screamed with fear. Just like my cousin when my grandmother pulled out her tongue."

"She pulled out her tongue?!" Hedgehog gasped.

"Yes, and my cousin screamed like mad," said Scary Fairy. "I can understand why. The right shoe, which my grandmother pulled the tongue out of, was still quite new and useless without it. Our grandmother can be quite nasty, especially on Thursdays. If it was a Friday she would definitely have pulled the tongue from the left shoe, which was old and shoddy. She is much more agreeable on Fridays."

Scary Fairy yawned.

"I'm sorry if I terrified you," she said, before picking up her blanket and leaving.

"Terrified?" Hedgehog protested in a shrill voice. "Never."

Rompus Boo

Dormouse at least must be brought to his senses. Hedgehog decided on Thursday, as evening approached. Meanwhile, Dormouse was taking a nap.

"Get up, a fight is looming," Hedgehog yelled into his ear. "Skunk, Wild Duck and Mole are behaving as if this was none of their business."

"What business?" Dormouse yawned.

"Scary Fairy! For the last three days she's been collecting strawberries and wild cherries!"

"Perhaps she's making jam," Dormouse suggested, yawning and stretching.

"That's exactly what Mole said," Hedgehog pounced. "But he's not bothered by what happens to us. He will just burrow his way underground. What about us?"

"I haven't the faintest idea what you're on about," Dormouse said quietly.

"Of course you don't," screamed Hedgehog. "Because in this forest nobody gives an acorn about anything. All you care about is your stupid little selves. I tell you, Dormouse, she's been collecting bear pears and cat grass for a week now. Don't tell me she intends to decorate her hole with them!"

"You really are annoying," Dormouse said as he reluctantly followed Hedgehog out, hoping to get some peace and quiet later on.

On their way they bumped into Squirrel.

"Dear Squirrel," Hedgehog announced haughtily, "if we don't act immediately we're done for."

"I knew it," Squirrel said apprehensively. "This strange feeling has been haunting me. It started in the middle of the night. And now this."

"Hush," Hedgehog ordered, as they approached Scary Fairy's beech tree. They crept under the pine tree opposite her hole. There was a little screen of pine cones to hide behind, which Hedgehog must have built a while ago. Noticing the discarded pear pips lying all around, Dormouse concluded Hedgehog must have been spying on Scary Fairy for quite some time.

Scary Fairy was busy arguing with dandelions and scolding bramble thorns. "Don't you know that stinging and scratching aren't very nice? Just think what Owl would say."

"It doesn't help to be nice, whatever Owl says," she sighed. Tired, she climbed onto a swing and let her legs dangle freely, all the while thinking of her grandmother's china cups. She muttered to herself: "Tomorrow, hopsasa, tomorrow, tralala, tomorrow my Rompus Boo will come."

"Did you hear that?" Hedgehog hissed. "Rompus Boo is coming."

"Who is coming?" Squirrel shuddered.

"He must be quite rough," Hedgehog said. "I imagine he carries a big stick with him, and traps for animals."

"Don't get carried away," objected Dormouse.

In the meantime, Scary Fairy had collected quite a bit of moss. "I hope they will all come," she said to herself, "all the animals. Otherwise it will be a terrible Rompus Boo. I really must try very hard to get them all here."

"It must be a trap," Squirrel quivered. "Rompus Boo will gobble us all up. And chew us up. And swallow us."

In the evening, Hedgehog called a meeting.

"Hedgehog," Snail summed up the situation, "we all know that Scary Fairy can be nasty if she wants to be. But your accusations have gone too far."

Just at that moment Scary Fairy hopped out from behind the tree. In no time at all she had delivered a pile of violet envelopes to all the animals. She collected some goldenrod while she was at it and then vanished.

The meeting immediately broke up. All the animals were so curious that they couldn't wait to tear open their letters.

"*Dear Dormouse,*" "*Lovely Squirrel,*" "*Esteemed Snail,*" and so on, was written on each of the envelopes.

Dormouse read the message contained in his invitation out loud: "*Tomorrow is the day! I have baked bear pears and dog cherries. You'll also be served blackberry juice and mint milk. Come as soon as you wake up.*"

"My message is exactly the same," said Snail. Skunk, Jay and all the others said theirs weren't any different.

"I'm certainly not going to drink any sludge made from goldenrod," Hedgehog announced sarcastically. "No way. When

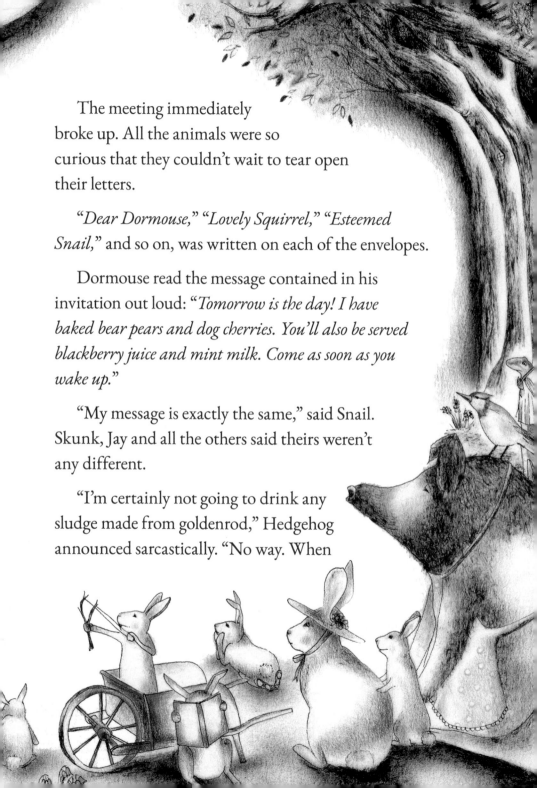

we're there, Rompus Boo will do us all in. Scary Fairy will bring her sisters, cousins, aunts and aunties. They will move into our homes. They will eat our hazelnuts! And chestnuts! And mulberries! And strawberries!"

There was a hesitant murmur of agreement from the animals.

"And in case you haven't heard, Owl and Bear can't be found," Hedgehog declared ominously.

"Woodpecker has combed the entire wood. They must have been eaten already."

Woodpecker felt obliged to nod.

"The only action left to us," said Hedgehog, climbing onto a tree stump so that the animals at the back could hear him as well, "is to drive Scary Fairy out of the forest."

Dormouse suggested that they should first get some sleep. Then, early in the morning, before the arrival of Rompus Boo, they would march to Scary Fairy's tree hole. Everybody agreed, except Hedgehog. The night was restless and full of nightmares.

.⁕.✂:✿⁕. .

The next morning the animals gathered, half-angry and half-frightened, in front of Scary Fairy's tree hole. "Scary Fairy!" Hedgehog shouted. There was no reply.

Hedgehog looked around for a tree stump. There wasn't one, so he climbed on a wood pumpkin instead.

"It's like this," he started, but was that moment overcome by a fit of nervous coughing. After all, driving Scary Fairy out of the forest wasn't a pleasant thing. And Hedgehog wasn't entirely without feelings.

"The fact is . . . " he started again.

Scary Fairy stuck her tousled head out of the hole.

" . . . that we wish you all the best for your Rompus Boo," shouted Owl and Bear, who were approaching with a large present.

"What's going on?" Hedgehog sneezed.

"What?" the animals repeated, astonished.

"Scary Fairy is celebrating her Rompus Boo today," Bear explained. By that time Scary Fairy had already slid down the tree and was tearing the yellow wrapping paper off her present.

"You mean to say some sort of birthday?" inquired Dormouse.

"It is the day little scary fairies bury their first gold coin," explained Owl. "From then on they celebrate the event every seventy-seven weeks."

"And receive presents," Bear said, looking around and frowning as he saw the other animals had come empty-handed. "Hedgehog, didn't you receive the message?"

"We nailed it to your door," said Owl.

"We explained everything," added Bear, as Hedgehog began to look more and more uncomfortable.

"We asked you to pass the message on," Owl looked at him sternly.

"Well, maybe I wasn't at home," Hedgehog mumbled and blushed.

"Wool slippers!" exclaimed Scary Fairy with delight as she removed the lid from the box.

"We had them made by the sheep," Bear proudly explained.

"Actually we got them in exchange for Hedgehog's bad temper," Owl said without blinking.

"What?" Hedgehog jumped. Everybody laughed.

"Won't there be a cake?" Boar asked.

"No," said Scary Fairy. "Rompus Boo is not celebrated with a cake but with a competition to see who can tell the scariest story."

Owl agreed to tell the first story.

She was about to start when
Squirrel jumped up. "I had a nasty feeling in the
middle of the night that something scary was going to
happen. Squirrel can't bear this anymore!" And she shot off like
a bolt. The competition commenced, with each animal in turn
recounting the scariest story they could think of. They were so
frightening that the rabbits, old as well as young, along with
Skunk and Snail, all terrified out of their wits, sloped away.

Next it was Salamander's turn to dash off in horror.

"Horror stories, I beg you," he muttered to himself
indignantly as he fled, displeased with the crowd's inferior taste.
He was one of the few salamanders who preferred poetry.

Even the fearless were soon too terrified to hang around any
longer. Only Hedgehog, Dormouse and Scary Fairy were left to
carry on. And then Scary Fairy told such a hair-raising story that
even Hedgehog and Dormouse made their escape.

"Such a wonderful Rompus Boo," Scary Fairy sighed
when she was finally left alone. "We had so much fun. And
never before have I won at scary storytelling! It was always my
grandmother—no one could ever defeat her."

Remembering her grandmother's stories, Scary Fairy
trembled with fright. She climbed into her bed and pulled the
duvet up to her nose.

How Hedgehog
Caught Rabies

One windy Wednesday Scary Fairy and Dormouse met under the oak tree. Dormouse was in a hurry.

"Hedgehog has fallen ill," he told Scary Fairy.

Scary Fairy remembered the pear Hedgehog had dragged as far as her tree hole the previous day. After saying that he was tired, he had left the pear and dragged himself home.

"I'll get the pear," she told Dormouse. Dormouse and Scary Fairy went their separate ways. While they were speaking, Snail had been slowly pulling himself along past the oak tree, a little too far away to hear the exact words. So instead of pear he understood spear. He wondered why Scary Fairy was getting the spear. Did she have a spear? And what did a spear have to do with a sick hedgehog? By the time he had pulled himself to the birch tree, where he met Mole, he was already very agitated.

"Scary Fairy has gone to fetch a spear because Hedgehog is ill!" he blustered.

"I'd better go and tell Owl," Mole
said as he leapt back into his hole.
He burrowed his way towards
the pine tree on which
Owl usually perched
during the day. But she
wasn't there.

Instead of Owl, Mole
found Woodpecker.

"Quick, find Owl," Mole said. "Scary Fairy is
threatening Hedgehog with a spear, just because he
is sick. I hope he hasn't got rabies," he added fearfully.

48

Woodpecker, completely confused, fluttered around the
wood until he ran into Dormouse.

"Have you seen Owl?" he screeched. "Hedgehog's got
rabies and Scary Fairy is about to attack him with a spear."

"Hedgehog!" shouted Dormouse through the window as he reached Hedgehog's abode. "Do you know what's wrong with you?"

"A bit of a sore throat, but it's much better now," Hedgehog replied in a good mood.

"That can't be right," Dormouse sighed. "You have rabies." He decided not to mention Scary Fairy and the spear; two pieces of bad news would be too much for Hedgehog.

Saddened, Dormouse departed. Salamander, who had been listening at the door, concluded that something had to be done.

When Scary Fairy dragged the pear to Hedgehog's cabin she saw Salamander nailing a notice on the door.

Under a drawing of a skull he had written:

NO ENTRY! BEWARE OF HEDGEHOG. HE
BITES!!!! HE'S GOT RABIES!

Scary Fairy wondered for a long time
what to do with the pear. After all,
Hedgehog must be hungry.

Salamander, who was often
in a poetic mood, wasn't this

time. He was terrified when he saw Scary Fairy knocking on Hedgehog's door.

"Can't you read?" he shouted.

Scary Fairy knocked again. From inside came a feeble voice: "Who is it?"

"Promise you won't bite me if I come in," said Scary Fairy.

"I can't even get out of bed, my legs are too weak," complained Hedgehog. "I'm done for."

Scary Fairy dragged the big pear into the cabin. She looked at Hedgehog for a long time. Then they both stared at the pear.

"Never again will I be able to carry a pear on my back," lamented Hedgehog.

"What nonsense is that?" asked Owl, who suddenly appeared at the door.

"I've got rabies," Hedgehog explained.

Owl laughed. "Who told you that?"

"Dormouse," replied Hedgehog.

"Woodpecker said so," said Dormouse, who was listening round the corner.

Woodpecker, perching on a branch nearby, got very angry: "Is it my fault if Mole invented the whole thing?"

Mole pushed his snout out of a nearby molehill and said: "I invented nothing. Snail told me. He also said that Scary Fairy was on her way to attack Hedgehog with a spear."

Snail couldn't defend himself, as he was pulling himself along the path on the other side of the wood. Owl looked at the pear and it gradually dawned on her what had happened. "Pear and spear don't even rhyme," she muttered to herself.

"Anyway," she said aloud to Hedgehog after touching his forehead with her wing, "you've recovered, I think."

Hedgehog was so glad he wasn't going to die that he jumped out of bed and suggested they all celebrate by eating the pear. Never before had he been so generous.

Scary Fairy Tames the Savage

It was late on a foggy Saturday. Scary Fairy was about to go to bed when Dormouse arrived in a rush and started to ROMPOMPOMPOMPOM on her door.

"Open up," he shouted. "It's a matter of life and death."

As soon as Scary Fairy unlocked the door, Dormouse barged in. He banged the door shut, bolted and locked it, and pushed a wardrobe against it.

"The Savage is coming," he announced, climbing into bed and covering himself with the duvet.

A terrible noise could be heard outside. Trees were snapping and branches were breaking.

"Hedgehog is out there," Dormouse said from under the duvet. "He won't survive this."

The noise subsided. Scary Fairy yawned and climbed into bed. But there was no peace.

ROMPOMPOMPOMPOM. Again someone or something was banging loudly on the door.

"Let me in," they heard Hedgehog screeching. "Or I'm finished."

Scary Fairy got out of bed, pushed the wardrobe out of the way, unlocked the door, and let Hedgehog in.

"Terrible," said Hedgehog, completely pale. "He hasn't bothered us for a year."

He quickly locked and bolted the door. He dragged the wardrobe back, pushed the table against it and climbed into bed next to Dormouse.

Again a terrible clamor and caterwauling could be heard outside. When it abated, Scary Fairy was so sleepy that she pushed her way under the duvet next to Dormouse and Hedgehog. She was about to fall asleep when there was another ROMPOMPOMPOMPOM on the door.

"It's the end," shouted Squirrel outside. "No one will survive. Poor Squirrel!"

Scary Fairy ignored Squirrel and pulled the duvet over her head so she could go to sleep. But Squirrel continued: "Scary Fairy! Listen to me, get up at once!"

Scary Fairy gritted her teeth and climbed out of bed. She pushed the table and the wardrobe aside and first unbolted then unlocked the door. She was nearly knocked over by the

animals that poured in, first Squirrel, then Skunk and finally Woodpecker. Just as she was about to close the door, Weasel along with a baby weasel also squeezed in.

"Terrible, horrible, spooky," they muttered. "Rampaging about like that. The nasty Savage!"

Squirrel locked and Skunk bolted the door. Weasel and her baby weasel pushed the wardrobe, the table and a chair against it. Then they all climbed under the duvet next to Dormouse and Hedgehog.

Morning was not far off. Scary Fairy should have been asleep a long time ago. But crowding her bed were Hedgehog, Skunk, Woodpecker, Weasel and her baby weasel, not to mention Squirrel and Dormouse. Only the very edge of the bed was still free. But not even the tiniest mouse could fall asleep on it. Every time Scary Fairy turned around, she flopped out of bed.

"Ohhhrrrggg," she gritted her teeth. But not one of her guests felt it necessary to climb out of bed and give her some space.

Scary Fairy went to the door. She pushed aside the chair, the table and the wardrobe. She unbolted and unlocked the door. She took her boots from the branch above, put them on and marched into the wood.

"She's gone crazy," Hedgehog said.

"She has a wild look about her," worried Dormouse. "Is this Savage thing contagious?"

"We must stop her," Skunk suggested.

Scary Fairy was marching straight towards the clamor coming from the Monstrous Abyss.

"Listen," Owl called from her tree hole, "you'd better go home."

Scary Fairy did not even look at her. And she didn't as much as raise her head when the South Wind dropped a large cone on her. All she muttered was "Get lost!" and marched on.

"We'll have to find Bear," Owl decided.

Scary Fairy strode straight towards the Monstrous Abyss and shouted: "Savage!"

The Savage grew even wilder, the ground trembled and the trees swayed madly.

"You're scaring my friends!" shouted Scary Fairy. "They're all hiding in my bed. If I don't get any sleep I'll be really cross tomorrow."

Suddenly there was silence and the ground stopped shaking. A slight rustle came from the undergrowth. *Snap, crackle.* First little claws appeared, then a disheveled head.

"You are the Savage?" Scary Fairy could not believe her eyes.

The little furry thing nodded.

"Why are you making such a racket and won't let us sleep?"

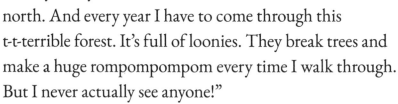

"I-I-I am a-f-f-fraid," stuttered the Savage. "Every year my Mum sends me on holiday to my aunt in the north. And every year I have to come through this t-t-terrible forest. It's full of loonies. They break trees and make a huge rompompompom every time I walk through. But I never actually see anyone!"

Suddenly Bear, Owl, Dormouse, Hedgehog, Skunk, Squirrel and Weasel with her baby weasel came rushing to the Monstrous Abyss.

"Here is your Savage," Scary Fairy yawned. The animals, too, couldn't believe their eyes.

"I got lost," the little Savage began to cry. "And I'm afraid of those who do rompompom in the trees. And those that squeal and shout. Most of all I'm afraid of the one that keeps shouting: 'We're done for!' I was afraid it would gobble me up if I stopped."

Dormouse, Hedgehog and Skunk felt a bit silly. Weasel and the baby weasel returned to their den. Owl and Bear were greatly relieved. Squirrel said: "You poor thing, Squirrel knows what it feels like."

"Come," Scary Fairy took the Savage by its furry hand. "First you will eat and then we will have a good night's sleep." And so, hand in hand, they shuffled off towards her tree hole.

Dormouse Wants to Set a World Record

On a completely ordinary Monday, Hedgehog began to reproach Dormouse for being lazy.

"You have no obligations," he kept on nagging from eleven till noon. "Not a care in the world."

Dormouse was taken aback and thought about this long into the night. The next morning he told Hedgehog, Squirrel and Scary Fairy: "I'm going to set a world record."

But what sort of record, he didn't yet know.

Hedgehog was angry that he hadn't thought of something like that himself.

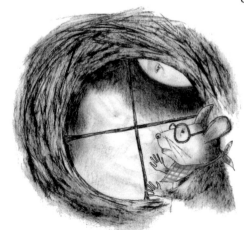

"You could set a record in painting," Squirrel blustered.

"You could climb the highest tree in Wicked Wood," suggested Scary Fairy.

Dormouse liked the idea. The highest tree was a poplar. As if for fun, Dormouse climbed all the way to the top. But no sooner had he come down than he saw Squirrel had also reached the top of the poplar tree.

"Yoo-hoo," she waved at them from above. "Look, I climbed even higher. I broke your record."

For a long time they sat quietly under the poplar tree. Then Scary Fairy had an idea: "Suppose you set the record for the number of times you can run round a very large oak tree?"

"That I could certainly manage," said Dormouse, and they looked for a very big oak tree. Dormouse got ready and set off. Squirrel ran after him. Hedgehog counted. "Twenty-two, twenty-three . . . " An hour later Dormouse was still running round the oak tree.

"Three thousand eight hundred and twenty-two, three thousand eight hundred and twenty-three," Hedgehog continued to count.

After circling the tree eight thousand five hundred and
thirteen times, Dormouse was quite out of breath and
Hedgehog was fed up with counting. After nine thousand
three hundred and five rounds, Dormouse could hardly
drag himself along. After the nine thousand three hundred
and sixth round he collapsed. Squirrel, who had followed

him round the tree, was also completely worn out. But she pulled herself together and managed to scrape in one more circuit. Then she collapsed.

"Squirrel broke your record again," remarked Hedgehog.

Dormouse was silent. After a while he recovered and got back on his feet. So did Squirrel.

Scary Fairy kept frowning and racking her brains. If I bite Squirrel's tail, she pondered, Owl probably wouldn't like it.

"You could break the record for moving trees," she suddenly remembered, determined to get rid of Squirrel.

"What?" exclaimed Hedgehog, Dormouse and Squirrel.

"If you moved the beech to where the oak is, and the oak to where the poplars grow," she winked at Dormouse. "In fact if you moved all the trees in Wicked Wood you would become a world champion in tree-moving."

Squirrel was overcome with anxiety. She would never find her hazelnuts again if Dormouse decided to move the trees.

"In my opinion that isn't a good idea," she said.

"I think it is," said Dormouse.

Squirrel said she wasn't having any of it and went home.

Dormouse, Hedgehog and Scary Fairy walked on. Hedgehog wasn't too happy that they had got rid of Squirrel so easily. Now Dormouse had every chance of setting a record. He began to complain that he was hungry and thirsty. That he couldn't walk any more. And that in this heat even ants couldn't breathe, let alone a beast like himself. In fact it was a very pleasant and fresh day, but Hedgehog nevertheless went on moaning.

"I should've stayed at home," he fussed, "you really do come up with some stupid ideas, Dormouse."

He wouldn't let up, and even demanded that Dormouse carry him. Dormouse had finally had enough. He stopped and gave Hedgehog a tap on his snout.

For a very long time afterwards they walked in silence. No one knew where they were going, and no one asked. They came almost as far as the source of the stream. They climbed over large slippery rocks, some covered in moss. It was dangerous. It was exhausting. Hedgehog didn't as much as squeak.

Otter was standing on one of the rocks. She seemed to be a reasonable sort, although otters could be quite weird.

"Have you come to see me?" she asked.

"No, we have come to set a record," replied Scary Fairy.

"Good," said Otter, "but set it in such a way that it will be in tune with the surroundings."

"That was our intention," said Scary Fairy.

"You seem nice enough," said Otter, "so here is a piece of advice. Don't make friends with an otter if you don't have room for her wise remarks."

Then Otter disappeared among the rocks. The others looked at each other, puzzled.

Dormouse suddenly had an idea. "I'm going to drink up the whole stream."

"Drink up the stream?" frowned Scary Fairy.

"That'll be my record," explained Dormouse. "Squirrel won't be able to break it because the stream won't be there anymore."

"Don't be stupid," said Hedgehog.

Dormouse approached the stream. But the moment he opened his snout to start drinking, something flew out of the water and said: "Booooo!"

Dormouse was frightened almost to death.

It was Otter.

"You want to set a record?" she laughed, climbing out of the water.

"These rocks," she continued, "have been covered in moss for centuries. There was once a seagull. He flew all the way from the sea. He was very proud of himself. No seagull had ever flown so far. Then he left. But the rocks remained and the moss is still growing on them."

"This Otter," Hedgehog whispered to Scary Fairy, "is really odd."

"But she may actually be very wise," said Scary Fairy.

Otter yawned. "But," she continued, "one day even this stream and these rocks will pass away and be no more."

Then she slid back into the water and disappeared.

Otter's words made a deep impression on Dormouse. He turned around and went home. Now he had the answer. When Hedgehog next accused him of being lazy, he knew that this, too, would pass.

Scary Fairy Makes a Large Puddle

One terribly hot Tuesday in July, all the animals were holed up in their various homes. They were dreaming of cool breezes. The world had come to a standstill. The treetops had never been so motionless. Only damp humid air rustled among them.

Scary Fairy poured a can of water into a pot and soaked in it all afternoon. It didn't really help. The hot humid air enveloped the wood well into the night. Scary Fairy could hardly wait for the moonlight, when she could cool her feet in a puddle.

But when she got to the puddle it was already occupied by Boar and her six piglets. At the shallow

end a young male frog was doing his best to romance a lady frog. Woodpecker was jumping about. Scary Fairy could barely find a free corner for herself. But as soon as she did, something moved under her feet. It was Earthworm. He yelled: "Hey nasty! Watch your step!"

Scary Fairy went home. The unbearable heat lasted well into the next day and there was no sign that it was going to end any time soon. Scary Fairy went to see Dormouse.

"Not a breath of fresh air," he sighed.

"We'll have to build a swimming pool," said Scary Fairy. "It's the only way."

Dormouse considered this for a while. Then he said: "Let's go and ask Beaver if he is willing to help."

Beaver lived on the other side of Wicked Wood. He was a lazy and rather odd beaver who spent most of his time lounging in a frazzled armchair. He disliked company. The thought of having to chat to someone over tea and biscuits made him scowl.

Scary Fairy knocked on his door.

Beaver closed his eyes and pretended to be asleep. He had no intention of opening the door.

"The heat is unbearable," said Scary Fairy when she got tired of knocking, opened the door and barged in uninvited. "You'll have to build a dam!"

Now Beaver had no other choice but to open his eyes. Standing before him was a silly little girl who just wouldn't stop pestering him.

"The puddle has dried up," she fretted.

"The earth is scorched," she went on.

Beaver wanted to tell her to stop bothering him with such nonsense. But for him that would have meant too many words.

So he simply said: "Shush, get lost!"

But Scary Fairy stood her ground. "None of us can cool our feet anywhere. Not me, not the frogs, nor Boar with her piglets, and not even the rabbits."

Beaver had to get up and assume a threatening posture before the little creature and Dormouse left.

"Damn nuisance!" he muttered as he went to close the door. Then an idea suddenly occurred to him: "You know what? I'm going to build a dam. I haven't done that for years."

Later that day Squirrel, Dormouse, Hedgehog and Scary Fairy were sitting on the cracked earth when it all started.

First Mole was shot out of his molehill by gushing water.

"Flood!" he yelled. "Water has filled all my passages."

Then the rabbits bolted out of their holes, of which there were quite a few.

Slowly, water began to spread across the whole forest, drowning the cracked earth, the dry grass, all the dust of the summer, and all holes and cavities. The level kept rising.

"We'll have to start a rescue operation," said Bear once he had managed to wade to Owl's place.

"Yes," Owl nodded, "quite a few have lost their homes in the flood. Fortunately Mole and Hedgehog are safe with Dormouse. The main problem is with the rabbits. For the time being we have put them up in the branches of the old oak tree. But I have no idea what to do with Boar and her piglets."

"Let me help," said Bear.

Boar and her six piglets were moved to the top of a magnificent beech tree. A scaffold was made for them, and even a fence. But Boar, who was scared of heights, was hysterical.

"We'll fall off! Don't you hear me, we'll fall off!" she kept shrieking.

"It's strange, isn't it?" Owl said on the third day of the floods. "I mean, there wasn't any rain."

"True," Bear agreed. "Why doesn't the water recede?"

Scary Fairy blushed and then dove into the water. That was her thirteenth jump that morning.

"Soon we'll run out of food for the piglets," Owl said. "Not to mention all the young rabbits."

Squirrel came paddling past in an upturned umbrella. She was collecting the hazelnuts and acorns that were floating on the surface of the water.

"We're all going to die of hunger," she said darkly.

It was Dormouse who first saw the large wooden box that came floating past the tree trunks.

The word ARMY was written on it.

"There is
nobody called Army here,"
Squirrel said angrily. "It has been sent to the
wrong address."

"What you don't possess not even the
army can take away," Hedgehog muttered,
remembering something he had heard before.

Only Scary Fairy thought to actually open
the box.

"Nothing but cheese," she said as she lifted
the lid. "It probably was meant for us."

The cheese tasted good.

"It's really kind of Army," said
Dormouse as he noticed another box near
the pine tree.

Inside were many pairs of large black boots.
WATERPROOF was written on them.

"Army has thought of everything," Owl said
excitedly. "Let's give them to the young rabbits
so they can float about in them a bit."

More boxes came floating past. Sitting on one of them was a toad that no one had seen before.

"The warehouse was flooded," Toad explained. "It seemed like a unique opportunity to see the world. It's very nice here."

"Have you seen Army?" Hedgehog wanted to know.

Toad nodded.

"What is it like?"

"How to put it," wondered Toad. "Army is one, but it has many." And off she went, floating away on top of the box.

"Army must be some kind of goddess," said Scary Fairy as she started to open the next box. "If there is nothing she takes nothing, but when she has many she takes care of everybody, including us."

She pulled a sheaf of maps from the box marked MAPS. They were all rather wet.

"What can we do with those?" Hedgehog grumbled. "Not too clever, this Army. It doesn't even know that water destroys paper."

"Shut up," said Squirrel. "Insulting Army is not a good idea."

"Look, lights!" exclaimed Scary Fairy as she pulled out some light sticks from the bottom of the box. And she read: "For marking dangerous spots, for reading maps in darkness, last three to eight hours."

"Not as stupid as you think, this Army," Scary Fairy turned to Hedgehog. "Afraid that we might get bored because we can't go anywhere, it has sent us maps together with lights, so we can read them."

"Thank you, Army," Dormouse shouted toward the sky, bowing respectfully. "Nice of you to send us all these things, but no offense, we'd rather not read now. It's hot and we would prefer to swim."

"Yes, it's high time the young learned to swim," said Scary Fairy. She tied all the boxes together into a long water train. "Dormouse, help me collect the young rabbits, bobbing about in the boots, they've paddled long enough."

"That won't be necessary," Bear waded up to them. "Beaver has built a dam, and that's why the wood was flooded," he explained.

"I had the feeling it was something like that," nodded Owl.

"I have demolished the dam," said Bear. "And in a few hours the water will be gone and you'll all be able to return to your homes."

Scary Fairy was distraught.

"But we were having such fun!"

"I know you were," Bear consoled her, "but some have been forced to leave Wicked Wood and are desperate to return."

That didn't help.
Scary Fairy started to
weep. She disappeared into her tree hole
and wouldn't come out no matter what.

"It's never all right for everybody," Owl
comforted Bear.

Rather depressed, they watched the waters recede.

Late in the evening Dormouse and Hedgehog came to fetch Scary Fairy.

"This you simply must see." They dragged her through the drenched wood. "It's true that the water is gone," Dormouse chuckled. "But look!"

They stopped at the meadow where the ground sloped inwards, so the water wasn't able to flow away. What lay before them was the biggest puddle anyone had ever seen in Wicked Wood. It covered the entire meadow.

Bear and Owl hung the light sticks sent by Army on the nearby trees. Meanwhile the young rabbits decorated the wood with pieces of colored string they had found in the last box.

All the animals then rushed into the puddle for a great midnight splash.

"Yoo-hoo," Scary Fairy joined them, delighted.

Soon Boar appeared and started to hand out ice cream cones to the young. When the reflection of the moon appeared on the surface of the big puddle they all grew quiet.

"What a night!" Hedgehog exclaimed.

The South Wind Encounters the Bora

One uneventful Wednesday, as the air began to smell of autumn, the South Wind decided to go on a trip. It came back with all sorts of things.

"Give me that," Scary Fairy jumped into the air and tried to grab a smart lady's hat from the South Wind's hands.

But the wind deposited the hat high in the upper reaches of a beech tree. Among the branches of an oak tree it left an old cuckoo clock, and a lovely china teapot could be seen swaying on a branch of a birch tree.

"Hey," shouted Scary Fairy. "Why don't you bring me china teacups? The ones with a rim

that's thinner than paper, and with the head of a queen at the bottom?"

In reply the wind shook the treetops and blew a leaf off the antlers that grew out of her cap.

"I bet you wouldn't dare," shouted Scary Fairy. "You're afraid, ha ha, afraid of my grandmother!"

Just then the horrible cold North Wind, known as the Bora, rose from the Monstrous Abyss. The South Wind tried to escape, but the Bora was stronger. Scary Fairy ran to the fern under which she had buried her gold coin. She kept digging and digging until it was all black under her nails.

The South Wind was screaming and howling. The Bora had almost swallowed it whole.

"Quick," shouted Scary Fairy, grasping the gold coin in her hand, "hide inside the coin."

The South Wind summoned up its last warm breeze, broke free of the Bora's embrace and funneled its way into the gold coin.

"Bora Pandora," shouted Scary Fairy. She stuck her tongue out at the Bora and waved her gold coin in the air.

The Bora threw himself at her with all his might. He lifted her high in the air and flung her against the tree so that the gold coin fell from her tiny hand. Scary Fairy landed on the mossy ground below.

A little later Bear, deathly pale, knocked on Owl's tree trunk.

"Auntie . . . Scary Fairy . . . terrible," he kept repeating with a lump in his throat. "It was the Bora . . . it's horrible . . . "

Owl burst out of her tree hole.

"I fear she's in a very bad way," Bear moaned.

When Owl and Bear reached Scary Fairy's tree hole the other animals were already there.

Salamander, who happened to witness the terrible event, repeated the story for Owl's benefit.

"Then she was thrown to the ground," he concluded. "And the Bora disappeared with her gold coin."

Owl shook her head. "Scary fairies must never lose their gold coins . . . If she doesn't get it back in three days . . . " Owl fell silent and wiped her eyes with one of her wings.

"Why didn't you do something?" Hedgehog snapped at Salamander, who didn't respond.

Bear carried Scary Fairy to her little bed and Dormouse stayed with her. He refused to let anyone else come near her. He wanted to believe that all Scary Fairy needed was some peace and quiet, and that everything would be all right.

The animals organized a search party. They searched every inch of the wood, hoping that Bora had dropped the coin somewhere. Hedgehog was the most determined.

For two days and two nights they searched the wood. Meanwhile Dormouse kept straightening Scary Fairy's pillow and left her bedside only to fetch another blanket for her. She was getting paler by the hour and Dormouse thought she must be cold.

On Friday afternoon Owl was forced to make an emergency landing on a branch of the pine tree as her eyes had filled with tears. That's also why she couldn't see what was rushing towards the wood. All she heard was the rattling of china.

It was the South Wind who crashed straight into Scary Fairy's beech tree. Enraged Dormouse poked his snout out of his hole.

"What the . . . " he began, but immediately fell silent.

The South Wind paid no attention. It whooshed past him to Scary Fairy's bed and gently pressed the gold coin into her cold little hand.

Then it warmly circled her head for a while.

Later, when the animals discussed these events they couldn't agree. Was it because of the warmth of the wind or because of the gold coin that some color returned to Scary Fairy's cheeks? Or was it because of the extra blanket brought by Dormouse? But everyone agreed that she opened her eyes and chuckled at the wind: "Howlingwind! From now on you're to be known as the Howlingwind. Someone who has defeated the terrible Bora deserves to have a terrifying name!"

The South Wind gently rubbed against her hand and shook the bedside table so that the china cups rattled.

"I can't believe it," Scary Fairy exclaimed to the wind. She wanted to jump out of bed, but Dormouse wouldn't let her. "You nicked them! You actually nicked my grandmother's china cups, the ones with a picture of a queen at the bottom. Grandmother must be raging and cursing." She laughed and sniggered to herself, making Dormouse quite nervous.

"Off with you," Dormouse swept the wind out of the tree hole with a broom. "That's enough excitement for one day."

"Laughter is the best medicine," grinned Hedgehog, who was leaning against the bottom of the beech tree. But Dormouse gave him such a stern look that he fell silent. For three more days Dormouse wouldn't let Scary Fairy leave her tree hole.

Meanwhile the animals had calmed down. Never before had anything in Wicked Wood frightened them so much. "Poor Squirrel," Squirrel told the story to a passing sparrow on his way to the south. "This whole ordeal has filled her with such despair that she can't remember where she's hidden her hazelnuts!"

Scary Fairy Holds a Literary Tea Party

One depressing Thursday the weather turned miserable. Autumn was beginning to make Wicked Wood cold, wet and foggy. The animals were snuggled up in their lodgings. Some were already sinking into hibernation. The wind was gathering more and more things, and dropping them under the pine trees and among the bushes.

Scary Fairy was treading on the wet leaves that were stuck to the ground, thinking how beautiful this time of the year was. "Wet leaves are so wonderful! The best part of the year," it seemed to her. "I wouldn't exchange two spoonfuls of fog," she said to herself, "for all the hurly-burly of summer! Trees without leaves are much more to my liking." She reflected, "everything is so clear and exposed. No treetops to obscure the sky, no place to hide . . ."

BOOMF! Something hard slapped her on the nose. It was the large cover of an old book.

"F-A-I-R-Y-T-A-L-E-S," Scary Fairy spelled out the letters on the cover. She put the cover under her arm. "An excellent tray for my china cups," she decided. Then a sheaf of pages suddenly landed at her feet.

"Little Red Riding Hood!" she exclaimed, reading the top page. Soon Scary Fairy was lost in reading. Occasionally she started to bite her nails, but when she came to the end she complained: "Listen, Howlingwind, half of the story is missing! And the wolf is just about to eat the girl!"

She searched the bushes all the way to the Monstrous Abyss. There she found another sheaf of pages fluttering among the branches of the pine tree.

Reading on, she was relieved to learn that the girl and her grandmother were saved. She felt a little sorry for the wolf, though. She knew quite a few of them, and not one of them was as villainous as the one in the story. She read on about Sleeping Beauty and couldn't believe that she pricked herself on a spinning wheel. All the spinning wheels were supposed to have been destroyed by order of the King. But then it turned out that they had forgotten one in the attic! Again, many of the pages were missing. By this time Scary Fairy was really angry with the wind. "Can't you bring me a book that's in one piece?"

The South Wind rubbed against her and rushed off into the unknown. Soon it deposited the rest of the thick book at her feet. Suddenly it started to rain. Scary Fairy ran with the book cover above her head and all the pages under her arm to her tree hole. She didn't emerge until she had read all the fairy tales. Then she opened the door and peeked out into the woods. There was no one to be seen.

No joyful shouting, no quarrels, no pushing, no shrieking. She looked at her precious book of fairy tales. I'm going to share these stories with everybody, she decided.

"I know," she suddenly had an idea. "I'm going to organize a literary tea party."

She pulled some sheets of pink paper from a drawer and wrote polite invitations. *"Dear Hedgehog,"* *"Darling Rabbit,"* *"Esteemed Salamander,"* and so on. She then wrote the same invitation to each and every one of them.

> *"Come to my beech tree on Thursday evening. We are going to have a literary tea party. We are going to knock the moon out of the sky, ride dragons and catch birds by their tails."*

Scary Fairy

She put on her best dress. All day long the South Wind helped her dry the moss. She spread it carefully over the leaves so that her guests would not be uncomfortable. It was soon ten o'clock and no one had come. Then it was eleven o'clock and still all remained quiet. Offended, Scary Fairy went to see Hedgehog.

"At least you could've come," she reproached him. "I consider you a friend, you know."

"What? To knock the moon out of the sky? What if it fell on my back and broke my needles? That would be too high a price for friendship."

Scary Fairy then went to see Dormouse.

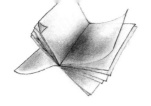

"I held a literary party today and you weren't there," she snapped at him.

"Oh," replied Dormouse. "You see, I've never ridden a dragon before. And to be honest, it doesn't sound like my cup of tea."

On the way home Scary Fairy met Wild Duck. Before she could ask her why she hadn't come, Wild Duck squawked at her: "You should be ashamed of yourself. Wanting to deprive birds of their tails, that's the last thing I expected of you!" Offended, she flew away.

For a few days Scary Fairy refused to come out of her hole. Then she started to write new invitations.

"Dear Stoat," "Darling Skunk," "Esteemed Boar," and so on. And then:

> *"Next Thursday evening you're invited to a literary tea party under my beech tree. I'm going to read you fairy tales about the princess who kissed a frog, the evil wolf and the three pigs (not suitable for children), and terrible thorns (an amazing tale about another princess)."*
>
> *Your Scary Fairy*

She delivered the invitations to all the addressees.

Thursday came round again. Again the South Wind helped her dry the moss, which had become very damp. She waited impatiently. Nobody came. They all shut themselves into their dens and refused to come out when Scary Fairy knocked on their doors. As she was returning home she met Frog and Boar.

"Unheard of!" Frog pounced on her. "To corrupt my tadpoles with sleazy tales about a princess and a frog. Shame on you!"

"Don't involve wild pigs in any of this," Boar got angry as well. "In any case, Salamander once organized a literary event and we had to listen to his tedious poetry for three hours!"

The next day when Owl flew over the wood she noticed a board in front of Scary Fairy's tree hole.

Written on it was:
BOAR KEEP OUT!

And another:
NO ENTRY FOR DORMOUSE!

And:
HEDGEHOG, KEEP OUT!

And:
SQUIRREL AND WILD DUCK, GET LOST!

And many other boards with similar inscriptions.

Owl knocked on Scary Fairy's door.

"Get lost!" shouted Scary Fairy. But Owl entered anyway.

Scary Fairy was furious. "I wanted all of us to have a great time, but nobody cares!"

Owl gave the matter some thought. She took the rest of the pink paper and helped Scary Fairy compose new invitations.

"Dear Squirrel," "Darling Boar," "Esteemed Salamander," followed by:

> *"Tonight I'm organizing a literary tea party.*
> *We're going to listen to wonderful fairy tales, spoil*

ourselves with sweet biscuits and have a great time.
All of you who want to spend an unforgettable
evening come to my tree hole at eight o'clock. We're
going to warm ourselves up with hot tea."

Scary Fairy

While the South Wind was delivering the post, Owl flew to Bear's den.

"Dearest Bear," she shook him awake, "I really would let you sleep, but if we don't do something Scary Fairy will be miserable and lonely for a very long time."

"Nothing good can come of that," Bear yawned.

At eight in the evening Bear and Owl dragged to Scary Fairy's tree hole not only Hedgehog, but also Rabbit and her young rabbits, Stoat, Squirrel and Wild Duck. Some, for example the entire frog family, came voluntarily because of the biscuits.

Without exception, they all agreed that they had an excellent time, that the fairy tales were out of this world, as were the biscuits, and that they would love to repeat the literary tea party the following Thursday. Only Salamander, with all his airs and graces, walked off in a pique.

Scary Fairy Says Goodbye

One depressing Sunday night Owl flew over Wicked Wood. The moon was shining and Scary Fairy was sitting by the side of a puddle. She was soaking her feet in the cold water. There was no joy, no jumping up and down.

"Are you ill?" Owl descended. "The moon is shining, but you're just sitting here."

Tears were gathering in Scary Fairy's eyes and there was a lump in her throat.

Owl stopped bothering her. She wasn't that sort. She flew off and left Scary Fairy alone. But she was worried.

She'll catch a cold if she keeps soaking her feet in the icy water, Owl thought. If this didn't stop before dawn she would have to wake Bear.

Next morning Owl, Dormouse, Hedgehog and Bear, although half asleep, could still hear Scary Fairy crying in her tree hole from far away. The South Wind was howling around her beech tree.

"Scary Fairy," Hedgehog gently knocked on her door. "Open up."

The little door opened and Scary Fairy pushed her head out, sniffling. She wanted to say something but then burst into tears. She gave the wind a dark blue envelope, which the wind passed to Owl.

Owl read:

"You have tamed the wind. You have served your time. So you can come home now. But don't forget my china cups! And my armchair!"

"It's from my grandmother," explained Scary Fairy. "I broke one of her china teacups, with a rim as thin as paper and with the head of a queen at the bottom. As punishment I was sent away. My grandmother said I would be allowed to return only when I'd tamed the wind. I thought she'd forgotten about me. And now this!"

The entire wood fell silent. No one, not Owl nor Bear nor Dormouse nor those who were listening in their dens and underground passages, knew what to say. Scary Fairy slowly started to pack. Dormouse and Squirrel helped her with the armchair.

"Of course you could always stay," said Hedgehog.

"Of course I could," said Scary Fairy. "But I'm cold. Winter is coming, and apart from my woolen slippers I have nothing warm to put on."

"We can get some wool from the sheep," Hedgehog was ready for action. "And Deer is very handy with knitting needles. And Stoat, too, could contribute some of his fur."

Scary Fairy started to cry again. "Howlingwind is very courageous but soon it'll be driven away by the North Wind, which bites to the bone. My tree hole is terribly drafty."

"It's only a store for hazelnuts," Squirrel explained apologetically. "Hazelnuts dry much better if they are exposed to drafts."

"You could spend the winter with me," suggested Dormouse. "You won't bother me in the least. I'll sleep all winter and won't even know you're there."

Scary Fairy sneezed, coughed and sniffed, and then said quietly: "I miss my sisters and cousins."

"You don't have to explain," nodded Bear, as he helped Scary Fairy fill the patched-up balloon with hot air. Everything had to be placed in the teapot. Then he helped her dig out the gold coin she had reburied under the fern. There was much work to be done. Scary Fairy gave her little mirrors to the young rabbits.

"You can have them," she said. "I really like you."

She was so sad she couldn't even look at Owl, Hedgehog, Bear, Dormouse, Squirrel, Stoat and Wild Duck. She waved to Boar and her young, and climbed inside the teapot. The balloon slowly rose into the air. Sadness, silence, despair and many other such things descended upon Wicked Wood.

103

"Hey," shouted Hedgehog when Scary Fairy was already high above them. "We don't even know your name."

"Hedgimilla," shouted Scary Fairy from under the clouds. "My name is Hedgimilla."

"Hedgimilla," repeated Hedgehog to himself. "What a beautiful name."

"It's good you asked," said Dormouse. "If she doesn't return we'll go and look for her."

"Yes, it's good you asked," Bear nodded. "How else would we find her among all those scary fairies?"